ASPEN COMICS PRESENTS

HOMECOMING™

VOLUME ONE

HOMEC

CREATED BY: MICHAEL TURNER, DAVID WOHL,
BRAD FOXHOVEN AND SCOTT LOBDELL

SCRIPT:
DAVID **WOHL**

PENCILS:
EMILIO **LAISO**

COLORS:
BRETT **SMITH**
WITH STEFANI RENNEE (PREVIEW, ISSUE ONE)
AND ANDREW CROSSLEY (ISSUE FOUR)

LETTERING:
JOSH **REED**

MICHAEL TURNER, DAVID WOHL, BRAD FOXHOVEN, SCOTT LOBDELL

HOMECOMING™ VOLUME 1

ISBN: 978-1-941511-18-3 FIRST PRINTING, REGULAR EDITION 2016. Collects material originally published as FCBD Preview Story and Homecoming 1-4

ISBN: 978-1-941511-17-6 FIRST PRINTING, COMIC BENTO VARIANT EDITION 2016. Collects material originally published as FCBD Preview Story and Homecoming 1-4

Published by Aspen MLT, Inc.

Office of Publication: 5701 W. Slauson Ave. Suite. 120, Culver City, CA 90230.

The Aspen MLT, Inc. logo® is a registered trademark of Aspen MLT, Inc. Homecoming™ and the Homecoming logo are the trademarks of Aspen MLT, Inc and Blockade Entertainment. The entire contents of this book, all artwork, characters and their likenesses are © 2016 Aspen MLT, Inc and Blockade Entertainment. All Rights Reserved. Any similarities between names, characters, persons, and/or institutions in this publication with persons living or dead or institutions is unintended and is purely coincidental. With the exception of artwork used for review purposes, none of the contents of this book may be reprinted, reproduced or transmitted by any means or in any form without the express written consent of Aspen MLT, Inc and Blockade Entertainment. PRINTED IN THE U.S.A.

Address correspondence to:
HOMECOMING c/o Aspen MLT Inc.
5701 W. Slauson Ave. Suite. 120
Culver City, CA. 90230-6946
or fanmail@aspencomics.com

Visit us on the web at:
aspencomics.com
aspenstore.com
facebook.com/aspencomics
twitter.com/aspencomics

ORIGINAL SERIES EDITORS:

VINCE HERNANDEZ AND FRANK MASTROMAURO

ASSISTANT EDITOR: JOSH REED

FOR THIS EDITION:

SUPERVISING EDITOR: FRANK MASTROMAURO

EDITORS: VINCE HERNANDEZ, ANDREA SHEA AND GABE CARRASCO

COVER DESIGN: MARK ROSLAN

BOOK DESIGN AND PRODUCTION: MARK ROSLAN

LOGO DESIGN: PETER STEIGERWALD

REGULAR COVER ILLUSTRATION: MICHAEL TURNER AND PETER STEIGERWALD

COMIC BENTO COVER ILLUSTRATION: EMILIO LAISO AND BETH SOTELO

FOR ASPEN:

FOUNDER: MICHAEL TURNER
CO-OWNER: PETER STEIGERWALD
CO-OWNER/PRESIDENT: FRANK MASTROMAURO
VICE PRESIDENT/EDITOR IN CHIEF: VINCE HERNANDEZ
VICE PRESIDENT/DESIGN AND PRODUCTION: MARK ROSLAN
EDITORIAL ASSISTANTS: GABE CARRASCO AND JOSH REED
PRODUCTION ASSISTANT: CHAZ RIGGS
OFFICE COORDINATOR: MEGAN MADRIGAL
ASPENSTORE.COM: CHRIS RUPP

To find the Comic Shop nearest you...

888-COMIC-BOOK
csls.diamondcomics.com
1-888-266-4226

GREEN HORIZONS
UFO INFO U NEED 2 KNOW

HOME HEADLINES ALIENS CELEBS CELEBALIENS ACTUAL NEWS

BLOG ABOUT WHAT'S IMPORTANT

> YES, CELESTE *DID* LIVE HERE BEFORE. UP UNTIL *TEN YEARS AGO,* TO BE EXACT.

> THAT WAS THE DAY SHE AND HER MOTHER DISAPPEARED FROM THIS HOUSE, NEVER TO BE HEARD FROM AGAIN... UNTIL NOW.

> AT THE TIME, AUTHORITIES SUSPECTED DOMESTIC VIOLENCE FROM AN EX-BOYFRIEND OF MOM'S, BUT NO EVIDENCE WAS EVER FOUND.

> THEY SIMPLY DISAPPEARED OFF THE FACE OF THE EARTH.

> THERE WERE SOME TABLOIDS THAT *DID* NOTE THERE *WAS* A UFO SIGHTING IN THE AREA AS WELL.

> GUESS THOSE THINGS *ARE* TRUE SOMETIMES, HUH?

> UNFORTUNATELY, WE WERE LEFT WITH A LOT OF QUESTIONS AND VERY FEW ANSWERS.

GRUESOME VIDEO SHOWS ALIEN BRUTALITY
crackdowns against anti-alien encounter groups continue across

HOTTEST VIDEO

Speach Jamming Gun

A new Speach Jamming Gun has been developed from Alien technology. 💬 12

CNN could not verify the authenticity

The alien bodies lay stuffed and tangled in the back of a San Diegoian pickup like garbage. 💬 10

How Much Do You Own Of Your Own Body?

Aliens probing stories from top celebs. 💬 68

Gover... Stalem...

Interes... 250 percent as the government finally decide something 💬 03

...bway on the Moon? ...hat's Next?

...new photos show an intense subway travel system on surface of moon 💬 138

Invisible Man enters Top Secret Facilities in Washington D.C.

An unidentified man wearing what appears to be an invisible cloak enters... 💬 12

Asteroid Heading for the United States

An asteroid the size of Texas is headed towards the United States right now. 💬 12

IN HILLCREST, MOTHER AND DAUGHTE...
eaceful town of Hillcrest is in an uproar...

> SHE DIDN'T REMEMBER MUCH BEYOND THAT SHE HAD SOME KIND OF JOB TO DO, AND SHE WAS STAYING ON EARTH UNTIL SHE DID IT.

The once peaceful town of Hillcrest is in an uproar over the mysterious disappearance of Carla Lee, 34 and ... een on June 4, the family's vanishing has put the ... e Chief Lenny Crupps said the department is inve... rick Raymundo, who is believed to be a... as well as battery and multiple charges of dis... in question, Raymundo has claimed he was home watching NBA's Los Angeles Lakers with his mother. Although Raymundo's alibi has been confirmed, he has been ordered to remain in the vicinity of Hillcrest, pending further inquiry.

> AND SHE HAD NO IDEA WHO THEY WERE, JUST THAT THEY WERE *SCARY.*

Police have refused to comment on reports of ... Object (also known as a U.F.O.), believed to have bee... nborhood on the night in question, but the department ... n calls during the period of 9 PM through 9:20 PM, v... tioning the area surrounding the Lee residence while describing the location of the U.F.O.

Renowned U.F.O. expert, Riley Martin, confirms that this has all the earmarks of a classic alien abduction, and he continued "I wouldn't be surprised if they popped back up some time in the future, with no mem... be honest, the same thing happened to me, about 30 ... And if what happened to me is any indication, I woul... poor little Celeste's shoes right now." Martin currentl... Sanitorium.

> WITH NO MONEY AND NO I.D. I COULDN'T JUST LEAVE HER ON THE STREET, SO I LET HER STAY WITH ME.

Whether the disappearance can be explained by alien abduction or nefarious a... committed by jealous boyfriend, this reporter suspects we haven't heard the la... of the Lees. If anyone has any knowledge of the whereabouts of mother or daughter, please contact our tip line at 1-800-PHONE-HOME.

> MY MOM WAS WORKING IN TOKYO AND WASN'T DUE BACK FOR *WEEKS,* SO THAT WASN'T AN ISSUE... FOR NOW.

SUBSCRIBE
/HomecomingComic

💬 12 Tags: *Alien*, *Missing*, *Spirits*, *Hillcrest*, *U.F.O.* Share: f t

PART ONE

PRIMM, NEVADA.

I TELL YOU, LADIES AND GENTLEMEN, SOMETHING'S IN THE AIR. I CAN *FEEL* IT!

RUMOR HAS IT THAT NASA HAS BEEN TRACKING UNIDENTIFIED OBJECTS IN OUR SOLAR SYSTEM *AS WE SPEAK!*

THIS IS TOM VINSON. HE'S WHAT YOU MIGHT CALL AN "ALIEN ENTHUSIAST."

LIVING IN "MODEST" ACCOMMODATIONS ON THE OUTSKIRTS OF LAS VEGAS, HE RUNS A WEBCAST DEVOTED TO ALL THINGS EXTRATERRESTRIAL.

THE ALIENS ARE *ON THEIR WAY* TO OUR BACKYARDS, MY FRIENDS, AND *OUR GOVERNMENT* KNOWS *WHEN AND WHERE* THEY'LL ARRIVE.

OF COURSE THEY WILL NEITHER CONFIRM NOR DENY, BUT FRANKLY THEY DON'T NEED TO. THE TRUTH IS ALL OVER THE WEB.

JOHNNY IN BARSTOW, IT'S *YOUR* SOAPBOX.

THANKS FOR TAKING MY CALL, TOM. I CAN SWEAR I SEE SOMETHING IN THE SKY RIGHT NOW. YOU SHOULD CHECK IT OUT.

TOM HAS ALWAYS HAD AN AFFINITY FOR THE SUBJECT...

I'LL BE DAMNED.

NO S#!$--I MEAN, EXCUSE ME, FOLKS. I'LL BE RIGHT BACK. IF WHAT JOHNNY SAYS IS TRUE, ALL OUR LIVES MAY CHANGE TONIGHT.

...PRETTY MUCH SINCE HE SAW *CLOSE ENCOUNTERS* TWENTY TIMES WHEN HE WAS SEVEN YEARS OLD.

THE SONOFABITCH IS RIGHT.

UP *YOURS,* NASA!!!

GROWING UP, WHEN HIS FRIENDS WERE DREAMING ABOUT BEING MICHAEL JORDAN OR BRAD PITT, HE FANTASIZED ABOUT ALIEN ABDUCTIONS.

WHEN HE LEARNED ABOUT AREA 51, HE BEGGED HIS FATHER TO TAKE HIM THERE FOR A FAMILY VACATION.

HE GOT SMACKED, INSTEAD.

...AND FOUND NOTHING BUT A BUNCH OF JUNKY GIFT SHOPS AND THE GRIFTERS WHO WORKED THERE.

EVENTUALLY, WHEN HE WAS OLD ENOUGH TO GET OUT OF THE HOUSE, HE HITCHED A RIDE TO ROSWELL, NEW MEXICO...

IN THE TWENTY YEARS SINCE, HE'S VISITED CROP CIRCLE SITES AND EVERY KNOWN LOCATION WHERE *UFOS* WERE REPORTED ON AMERICAN SOIL.

NEVER SAW A THING.

THWUMDK-SHHH

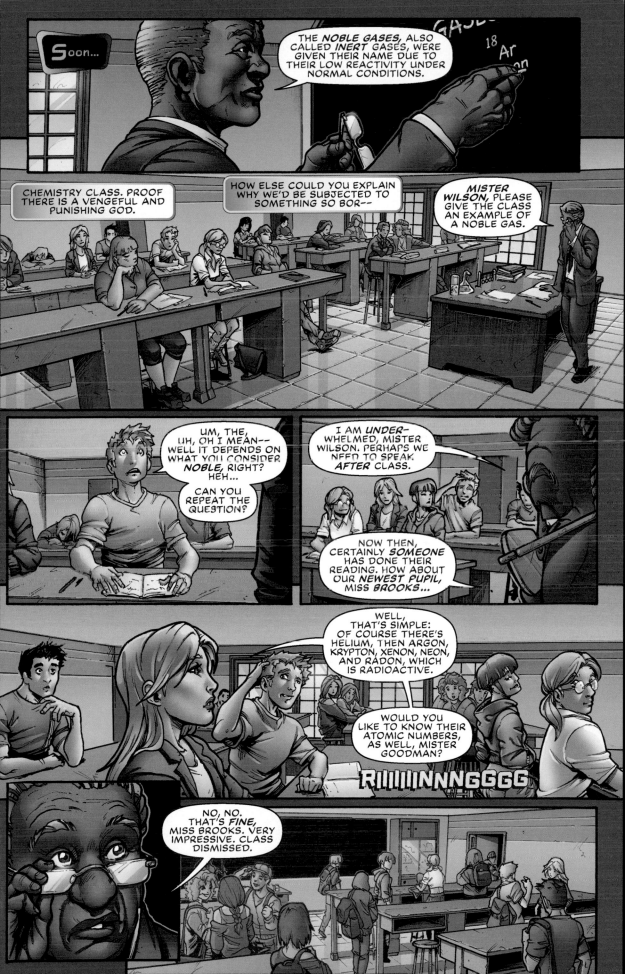

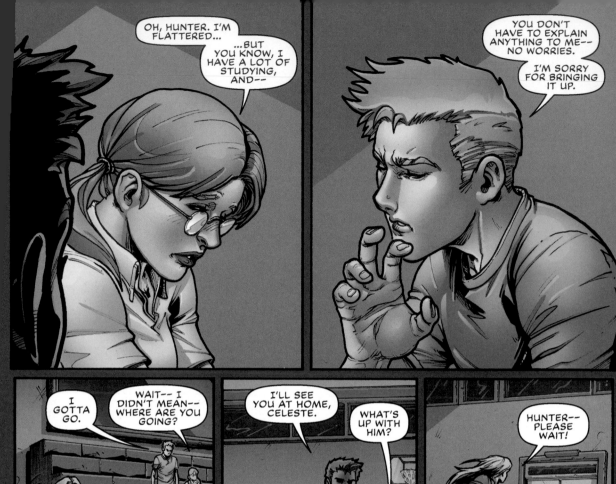

OH, HUNTER. I'M FLATTERED...

...BUT YOU KNOW, I HAVE A LOT OF STUDYING, AND--

YOU DON'T HAVE TO EXPLAIN ANYTHING TO ME-- NO WORRIES.

I'M SORRY FOR BRINGING IT UP.

I GOTTA GO.

WAIT-- I DIDN'T MEAN-- WHERE ARE YOU GOING?

I'LL SEE YOU AT HOME, CELESTE.

WHAT'S UP WITH HIM?

HUNTER-- PLEASE WAIT!

WHAT HAPPENED?

LOOK...I DON'T WANNA TALK ABOUT IT, ALL RIGHT?

I KNOW I DIDN'T HANDLE THAT SO MATURELY. BUT WHAT DO YOU WANT? I WAS HURT AND CONFUSED.

IN RETROSPECT, IT WASN'T THAT BIG OF A DEAL, COMPARED TO WHAT HAPPENED NEXT...

SKREEEEEEEE

PART TWO

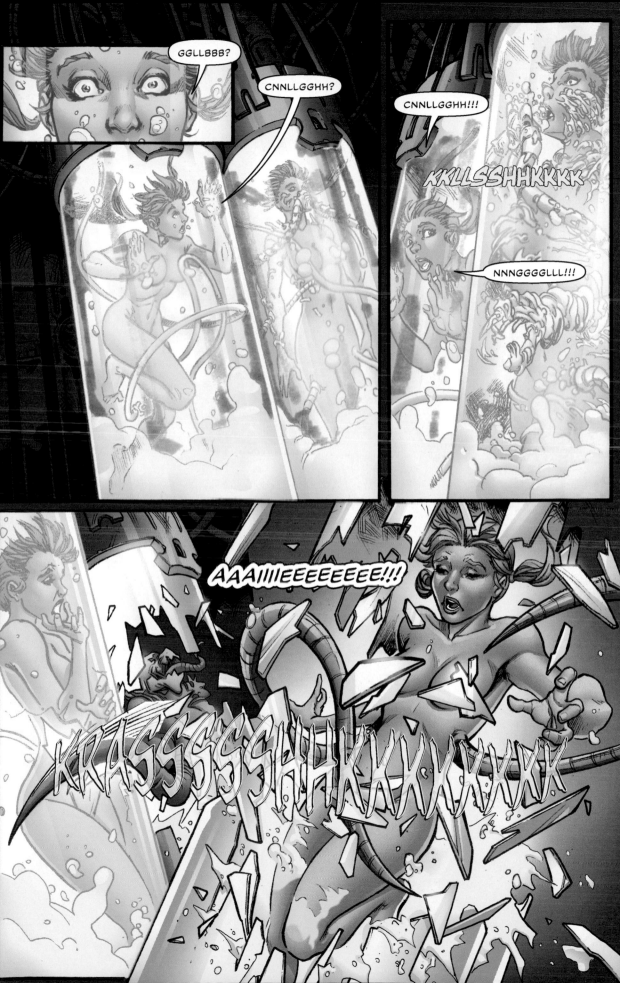

RIIIIIINNNGGGG

PLEASE BRING YOUR PAPERS TO THE FRONT OF THE ROOM.

HUNTER, YOU TELL MS. FINCH THAT SHE'D BETTER HAVE A *VERY* GOOD EXPLANATION FOR HER BEHAVIOR TODAY.

I'M SURE SHE'S SICK, MRS. FIORE. I-- UM-- YOU KNOW SHE *WAS* COMPLAINING OF STOMACH PAINS BEFORE--

BEEP

H--grab a jacket from your locker and meet me at girl's room-- NOW! Thx!

SHORTLY...

KNOCK

KNOCK

KNOCK

JAY ANNE, IT'S--

CLIK

WHUP

--ME?!?

HEY THERE, LADIES.

HAVE A NICE DAY!

SMOOTH, HUNTER.

JAY ANNE! ARE YOU ALL RIGHT?

I'M FINE.

FIORE IS *PISSED!*

I THINK I CALMED HER DOWN, THOUGH. TOLD HER YOU WERE SICK.

LOOK, JAY ANNE. IF THINGS ARE WEIRD FROM ME ASKING YOU OUT YESTERDAY... I JUST... WELL, EVERYTHING'S COOL, ALL RIGHT?

LET'S JUST GO BACK TO NORMAL.

HE DIDN'T...

HUNTER... EVERYTHING IS *NOT* COOL.

AND *NOTHING* IS *NORMAL* ANYMORE. DO YOU *REMEMBER* LAST NIGHT? DO YOU REMEMBER WHAT *HAPPENED* TO US?

WHERE IS YOUR *COUSIN?*

I NEED TO TALK TO *CELESTE.*

NEARBY...

SPECIAL AGENTS BRAISIN AND MACKIE, FROM THE HOMELAND SECURITY DIVISION OF THE SHERIFF'S DEPARTMENT, ARRIVED IN HILLCREST A SHORT WHILE AGO...

...RELUCTANTLY.

THEIR FIRST THOUGHT WAS THAT THIS WOULD BE A MAJOR WASTE OF TIME.

WHO'D WANT TO BOMB A SCHOOL GYM, BESIDES SOME DISGRUNTLED CHEMISTRY STUDENTS WITH A GRUDGE?

SEEMED UNLIKELY, BUT ORDERS WERE ORDERS.

AT FIRST, THE SEARCH YIELDED NOTHING MORE THAN A BUNCH OF DECORATIONS... UNTIL...

I'VE SEEN THESE THINGS ALL OVER. THIS LOOK LIKE A DECORATION TO YOU?

PROJECTILE, MAYBE?

MAYBE.

SOMETHING WENT DOWN IN HERE-- AND IT WASN'T FAULTY WIRING.

WE NEED TO TALK TO WHOMEVER WAS IN HERE LAST NIGHT...

...GET THE REAL STORY.

PART THREE

I'LL JUST PUT IT HERE.

MY GIRL. YOU WERE ALWAYS SO BRAVE.

BUT TELL ME-- WHAT HAPPENED TO YOU? WHERE DID THEY TAKE YOU?

TO BE HONEST, I STILL DON'T REMEMBER MUCH. IT COMES BACK IN FLASHES.

THEY NEVER HURT ME. THEY NEEDED ME. I WAS THEIR CONDUIT, I DON'T THINK THEY HAVE *BODIES.*

I *KNOW* THIS'LL SOUND CRAZY, BUT I WAS ON A MISSION-- PURSUING THEIR ENEMY. THEY CALLED THEM *REBELS* OR SOMETHING. THEIR SHIP CRASHED AND I...

...CAME *HERE.* WELL, OUT *THERE,* ACTUALLY. BY THE POOL.

I GUESS I WAS *DRAWN* HERE, BUT WHEN I ARRIVED I HAD NO IDEA WHY.

HUNTER TOOK ME IN. CLOTHED ME. ENROLLED ME IN SCHOOL. HELPED ME REMEMBER.

YOU'VE BEEN A GOOD FRIEND TO MY DAUGHTER-- AND NOW, TO *ME.* I WON'T FORGET YOUR KINDNESS.

IT'S NOTHING.

HUNTER IS MODEST, AS USUAL. HE STOOD BESIDE ME DURING THE FIRST STRIKER ATTACK THAT INJURED OUR FRIENDS.

IF IT WEREN'T FOR THE BIOJUVINATION CHAMBERS ABOARD MY VESSEL, I DON'T KNOW WHAT I WOULD'VE DONE.

THIS IS ALL SO... *UNREAL.* YOU HAVE A *SHIP?* WHERE *IS* IT?

IT'S... AROUND. BUT CLOAKED. PRETTY MUCH UNDETECTABLE.

IF YOU DON'T MIND ME ASKING, HOW DID *YOU* GET HERE, MS. LEE?

I-- OH, I'M SORRY. THIS IS ALL JUST TOO MUCH. MAYBE I CAN REST A BIT MORE AND THEN WE CAN SPEAK AGAIN.

OF COURSE, MOM. HUNTER AND I NEED TO GO TO SCHOOL ANYWAY. WE CAN TALK LATER.

COACH, DO WE *REALLY* NEED ANOTHER ROUND? EVEN *I'M* BEGINNING TO FEEL BAD. KINDA.

NO. FIRST TO *THREE.* LET'S DO THIS.

HE'S LOOKING UP-- *HEY PAUL!*

TRY NOT TO GET YOURSELF KILLED.

VERY SWEET.

I TRY.

AW, YOUR FAN CLUB SHOWED UP.

YOU GUYS GONNA GO *KNIT* TOGETHER AFTER I KICK YOUR ASS AGAIN?

FWEEEEEEE

YOUR FUNERAL, CAMPBELL.

SHOULD'VE QUIT WHEN YOU HAD THE CHAOOUUUULLGG HHH!!!

HNH?

SORRY TO DISAPPOINT YOU, CHARLES.

LUCKY F@#$. MUST'VE TRIPPED ME.

NEED A HAND?

JUST LINE THE F@#$ UP.

MEANWHILE...

HNH?

LIKE HER DAUGHTER CELESTE, IT HAD BEEN TEN LONG YEARS SINCE CARLA LEE HAD BEEN WITHIN THESE WALLS.

THIS PLACE, ONCE HER HOME, NOW SO DIFFERENT-- SO ALIEN-- IN EVERY WAY.

SKRITCH

KREEEEEK

ANY REMNANT OF WHAT WAS ONCE THE LEE HOME IS NOW LONG GONE.

KCHIK

JUST A DISTANT MEMORY.

SKRITCH

SKRITCH

ALL THAT REMAINS IS THE PAIN OF A TEN YEAR ORDEAL THAT FELT LIKE A THOUSAND LIFETIMES...

...AND A DARK SECRET THAT CARLA LEE CAN NEVER ESCAPE.

≷GASP!≶

TSSSSSS

AND IN THAT MOMENT, FORCED IT TO UNLEASH AN ASSAULT UPON ITS FELLOW STRIKER...

THIP THIP THIP

YEEEEEEEEEEE

...MUCH TO THEIR COLLECTIVE DISMAY.

FINALLY, ON THE VERGE OF EXHAUSTION, SHE SUMMONED THE STRENGTH FOR ONE LAST, GREAT BLAST...

KRRAKKOOSSHHH

...BANISHING THE NOW UNCONSCIOUS STRIKERS OUT OF THE HOUSE.

MOM...!

EVERYTHING WILL BE ALL RIGHT. I PROMISE.

SHE KNEW IT WAS RISKY, BUT PURSUIT WOULD NEED TO WAIT FOR ANOTHER TIME.

PART FOUR

IT'S ALL RIGHT, CELESTE. YOU'RE OKAY NOW.

I'M SORRY. I'M SO SORRY.

MY MOM-- SHE TRICKED ME TO GAIN ACCESS TO MY SHIP. SHE... CHANGED ME.

CAN SOMEBODY *PLEASE* TELL ME WHAT'S GOING ON HERE? WHAT IS SHE TALKING ABOUT? WHAT'S THE DEAL WITH YOU PEOPLE?

HONESTLY, DUDE, WE DON'T KNOW MUCH MORE THAN YOU DO.

ONE OF THOSE THINGS ATTACKED US, AND THE NEXT THING WE KNEW WE WERE ON A SHIP, HOOKED UP TO--

UH, PAUL?

YOU SHOULDN'T BE TALKING ABOUT THIS.

I THINK THEY *KNOW* SOMETHING STRANGE IS GOING ON, COLE.

WHAT SHIP?

OH...

COVER GALLERY

COVER A TO
HOMECOMING #1 by
• MICHAEL *TURNER* • PETER *STEIGERWALD* •

COVER B TO
HOMECOMING #1 by
• MIKE DeBALFO • MARK ROSLAN • PETER STEIGERWALD •

COMIC CON INTERNATIONAL: SAN DIEGO EXCLUSIVE COVER D TO
HOMECOMING #1 by
• EMILIO LAISO • BETH SOTELO •

COVER A TO
HOMECOMING #2 by
• EMILIO *LAISO* • BETH *SOTELO* •

COVER B TO
HOMECOMING #2 by
• MICHAEL RYAN • MARK ROSLAN • PETER STEIGERWALD •

COVER A TO
HOMEGOMING #3 by
• EMILIO *LAISO* • BETH *SOTELO* •

COVER B TO
HOMECOMING #3 by
• *Cory* SMITH • *Brett* SMITH •

COVER A TO
HOMECOMING #4 by
• Emilio *LAISO* • Beth *SOTELO* •

COVER B TO
HOMEGOMING #4 by
• KHARY RANDOLPH • EMILIO LOPEZ •

RETAILER INCENTIVE SKETCH EDITION COVERS TO
HOMECOMING by
• MICHAEL TURNER • EMILIO LAISO • MARK ROSLAN • PETER STEIGERWALD • BETH SOTELO •

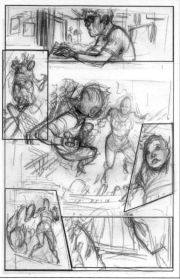

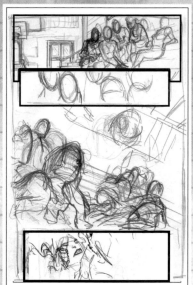
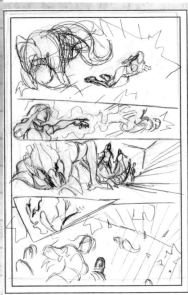

Initial Concept Sketch by • MICHAEL **TURNER**